THE VOID

THE VOID

D. ROGUE

Contents

PROLOGUE

People on Earth have different beliefs and theories about what happens after death, like Heaven and Hell, Reincarnation, nothingness, and all that jazz. Let me tell you now, they were wrong... kind of. The afterlife is somewhat of a combination of all those beliefs.

Heaven is a beautiful place, and all good people go there. However, after a week or so, they often think the world revolves around them (even though they're angels, it's still annoying), and Heaven is quite strict about its rules.

Hell is what they say it is, but the torture thing is no longer a "thing." They now schedule the time you are going to be tortured. Hell is now kind of like a rehab facility for people, and they have strong free Wi-Fi on Sundays (Only on Sundays, I mean, it's Hell); in

Heaven, you have to pay 60 gold coins to use your wings every three months.

Reincarnation can happen, but only after specific requirements are met. It's like getting a driver's license but with a lot of... not so PG stuff (if you're in Hell).

Now, there is this middle place in the afterlife, which they call The Void. It's a place where people go, who have been corrupted in any form or fashion when they were alive. But only so The Judges can figure out where to put the souls. This place is like a bustling city with blissful lights and beautiful scenery, but beneath this beautiful façade lies a terrible, creepy underworld of fear, evil, and death. YES, I SAID DEATH!

This is where my story begins, so please enjoy and have a good read of how I became the most feared thing in The Void.

~ IX

Chapter 1

A New Reality

"Augh, my head, where... where am I?"

I take a good look at my surroundings, and I'm surprised to see that I'm in something that resembles New York City's Times Square.

"Ok, I was in Atlanta a few minutes ago; what is going on here?!"

I was slightly scared, and as I was analyzing the situation, someone tapped my shoulder.

"HI THERE!"

I jumped back, startled to hear the voice of a young girl, and as I turned my head to see who was behind me, I saw a lady who looked to be in her late 20s to early 30s laughing.

"Sorry, I like to freak out the newcomers here," she says. I felt slightly confused and panicked, so I asked her, "Where am I? What is this place?!"

She laughed hard for a good while at that question.

"WHAT'S SO FUNNY? I WANT TO GO BACK HOME!!" I exclaimed.

She looks at me and says with the calmest expression on her face, "You are dead, and welcome to The Void."

At first, I didn't believe her, but as I looked around at my surroundings, I slowly realized this wasn't New York. All the buildings around me were black as charcoal, and some of their windows had white light shining through them. There were not many cars or other forms of Transportation, but there were still roads and highways. "Is this some sort of hot topic dimension?" I said, pointing towards the sky, which seemed to make the girl laugh even harder.

"So... is this the afterlife?" I said while still taking in the fact I was dead.

"I just told you it's The Void," she said with a confused face.

"What is The Void?" I asked, and she looked at me with a somber smile. "Let me answer that question with another," she said calmly. "What is your name?" I looked confused. "My name is..." I paused; I didn't know the one thing I had all my life: my name.

The girl looks at me sorrowfully, "That's how everyone starts here in The Void; they forget their name, how they died, and some even forget their entire lives when they were alive. It's a sad thing, but most of us move on and wait."

Now I stared at the girl and asked what her name was. "My name was the one thing I liked most when I was alive, cherries." I was jealous but also understanding, mainly because I felt we had gone through the same thing. "So, what now? I really don't know where or what to do here." Cherry's eyes lit up like a candle. I don't know why, but the way she looked felt familiar in a way.

"I know the perfect place to shop," she grabs my hand. After 3 hours of her making me run more than I could handle, we arrived at "THE H&H MALL.

"Oh, this is my favorite place to shop," she said with a cheerful voice. I felt a sense of nostalgia, but it faded away as soon as I saw what was inside the mall.

"HOLY SHIT!" I said as I looked in astonishment at the assortment of weapons, dresses, bombs, jewelry, and even more things. "This is bigger than it looks." But Cherry said not to question it, so I put it aside, albeit unwillingly, and then she abandoned me in the mall to look for dresses and other things.

I really liked the weapons aisle; it had all kinds of items, but the one that interested me the most was the scythe. I don't know why, but when I held it, it felt the most natural to use; the same thing for every other weapon I had in my hands, but not as much as the scythe.

I went to find Cherry but speak of the devil, she appeared out of nowhere.

"Hey~, did you miss me?" she said as she walked over with a shopping cart full of dresses and ammunition.

"So, the first weapon that I'm going to buy you is a scythe!?" She says, shocked and confused. "Well, we're already dead, right? Might as well look the part," I say jokingly. "Plus, it's not like we can die again."

She looks at me, sweating bullets. "Well, about that..." I turned to look at her.

"WE CAN'T DIE AGAIN, RIGHT!?" I say in disbelief.

As I'm freaking out, she puts her arm around my shoulder. "Calm down, let me explain. People can still die in this world, but after a certain time frame, you reform in the apartment you were given; check your left pocket." I put my hand in, feeling around, and felt a metal object. When I pulled it out, it turned out to be a key.

"How did I not feel this in my pocket till now?" I asked, questioning if my pockets were bottomless.

"Well, they don't appear unless you want them to, mainly so nobody can just steal your key, break-in, and kill you, but also, the timeframes are random. Most people take about 1 hour to 24 hours to reform in their apartment. It's rare ever to find someone who can reform in 10 minutes; that's the fastest recorded reform time in The Void." As I took in this information, I thought to myself, how long would it take for me to reform?

After she bought me my scythe (along with her stuff), we walked back to our respective apartments, and I asked her if she could also buy me a sidearm, but she said she had that covered.

Chapter 2

The Perfect Weapon

We had just left the mall, so idk (I don't know) if we were going to another mall or some black market shop.

"Welcome to my apartment; it's pretty neat, right?" Her apartment looked like a condo, but it also had a few flaws here and there; for one thing, her bedroom smelled like rotten eggs.

"So, a sidearm, right?" She stated. I nodded. "Well then, pick your Poison." She opened a closet full of Guns, Clothes, and

Money; as I looked upon the assortment of weapons deep inside, I felt excited.

I looked through the assortment of guns, mainly the ones that intrigued me the most. I weighed the pros and cons of each weapon, from assault rifles to pistols. I studied them all, plus some lessons about each type of gun from Cherry. So, I opted for two pistols due to them being small and suitable for close-range combat, along with the fact that I could hold two of them at once.

I chose 2 Glock 19s because they looked cool and because they were the only ones Cherry had holsters for. After finding some clothes to wear out in combat (a Cloak, a Black T-shirt, and Black Yoga Pants), I decided to see what my apartment looked like. I said goodbye to Cherry and went on my way. She was on the tenth floor. I was on the five hundredth floor, which still puzzled me.

After taking the elevator, I reached room number 121, which was the number labeled on the key. I opened my door to see a simple bedroom with posters on the wall, a computer, and a mini fridge. I lay down in my bed and go to sleep, thinking of what will happen tomorrow and everything I learned today.

***

I woke up the next day and did what I felt natural. I got up, ate some food, and watched what they call Voi-tube in this world (it still contains all the YouTube videos but also features additional content from people in The Void). I saw Cherry on my Beanbag chair, as I was about to go out...

"WAIT, CHERRY, WHAT ARE YOU DOING HERE," I said with astonishment. "What do you think? I know how to pick a lock," she said with a hint of laughter in her voice.

"Ok, so what do you want?" I said as she ate half of the breakfast I made in the microwave (it was on top of the mini-fridge).

"Well... I was going to... find you for... a raid, but..." I grabbed her food and put it in the trash.

"Now you can speak clearly, right?" She looked at me with annoyance and sighed.

"You didn't have to throw my food away, but ok, I was going to find you for a raid, but then I...." She goes on an hour-long tangent about how she got here.

"Ok, but what is a raid?" I asked her with curiosity.

"Well, a raid is when you go after a bounty or capture territory with a group of people, and the money is split between the group automatically."

I understood that, but then I realized something: "Um... I'm broke." She laughed a bit and said, "Don't worry, everyone who enters this world gets a set amount of money, but once you run out, you can't reform until you get some cash. One dollar will be enough to do so.

I was slightly surprised and said, "So money allows you to reform? If you have no money, you're dead?"

She nodded her head in affirmation as I got up to pick up some trash I had left around the apartment last night. She got up and turned to the door while saying, "I believe the raid should start in an hour, so if you're coming, you'd best tell me now."

I thought about it for a few minutes before agreeing to join Cherry. I grabbed my weapons and prepared for battle, and I had the same feeling of familiarity as last time. My lack of memory confused me, but I still wondered why all this felt so familiar to me. We walked for 4 hours to this rundown shed in the back of an alleyway in the city.

As we enter the shed, I see three people inside. "Let me introduce you to the crew," Cherry said.

The first guy was Lust. He said from what he could remember from when he was alive, he was a cultist, and he seemed to worship the Queen of Lust, whoever that is.

The second guy's name was Deviant; he told me that, from what he could remember, he had been a spy back when he was alive, and it was his codename. When I asked which government he worked for, he said he didn't know.

The third guy's name was Steve... it was his name when he was alive. The only reason he remembered it was because he was yelled at a lot throughout his entire life.

"So, what's your name?" Lust said with curiosity, "I-I don't know." I said, with nervousness in my breath.

"Not again, Cherry. I keep telling you not to bring newbies to the crew; he won't last 3 seconds on the battlefield." Deviant said with annoyance and worry.

"Well, I could... try to find a name." Everyone looked at me.

"Are you sure you want to do this? It's not going to be a walk in the park; you could be asleep for," Cherry interrupted Steve, putting her arm around him.

"I'm sure it'll be fine; we've got your back. Plus, if it's as lame as Steve's, we can make fun of 'em." Everyone laughed except for Steve, "Yeah, yeah, just get on with it, will Ya?"

I was surprised by the Boston accent, but I immediately asked Cherry in private outside...

"How do I find my name?"

She whispered in my ear, "Just try to meditate and think about what your name was; that's how I found mine."

The feeling of heat enveloped my entire body as I began meditating, with the scent of ash making it difficult to catch my breath. "Am I... tired?" I thought to myself, 'I was unable to see anything; it was like looking into a pitch-black void.' "How could you... Anubis..., I thought we were comrades?" A soft voice said sorrowfully. Just as suddenly as I fell asleep, I felt myself tugged DEEPER.

***

I open my eyes, sweating, and I look up to see them all, weapons drawn, except for Steve, who is terribly making pineapple margaritas.

"Wow, that was fast," Lust said.

"I thought it would take longer," Deviant said, annoyed, holstering his weapon and sitting in a more relaxed state.

"How long was I out?" I asked everyone, mentally exhausted after what I went through.

"Four hours," said Steve with annoyance.

"How long did it take you guys? "

"5 days," Lust said; "1 month," Deviant said; "2 days actually," Steve said; "12 hours," Cherry said.

I realized that, based on the timeframes, I had the shortest amount of time in the group to get a name from my memory.

"So what was the memory like?" Lust asked.

I tried to remember it, but it came up blank; only one word rang through my head." I... don't remember; all I can remember is the word Anubis.

"Everyone there had that same sorrowful look that Cherry had when she asked for my name.

"Don't worry, it will come back to you soon," Lust said, looking happy as he reassured me, but I knew he was only trying to comfort me. I wondered how long it took for them to remember the memory of where they got their names from, but I didn't dwell on it... because I felt like I was going to die if I did.

So, my name is Anubis? I thought to myself. Then I asked Lust what it meant.

Lust said that was from Egyptian mythology, but that's all he could remember.

I was proud that my name was related to a god, and the things I didn't understand started to make sense, from knowing how to use most of the weapons I held to not feeling any discomfort while preparing for fights, and now having a name related to an Egyptian god. I wonder who I was and why I have all these memories but no clues of who I was... or who I am.

"So, here's the plan to upgrade our area." Cherry said with a grin on her face, "We are going into Zone 20 and trying to capture one of their buildings on the barrier and make it our own without getting caught." Cherry said like a commander

"Steve, Deviant, you guys are going to switch shifts with the guards. Deviant, you know what to do; Steve, you'll be there as extra support."

"Roger," Steve and Deviant said firmly.

"Lust, you take your loudest gun, tank, whatever. Just keep them away from us for a few hours."

"On it," Lust said with his voice being in a high pitch, which I think was a joke.

"Anubis and I are going to capture the building."

"Ok... wait, WHAT?" I said, scared and surprised. "You must be crazy to bring me; I have no combat experience," I said, mainly due to my gut telling me not to go with her.

"Well then, I'll protect you because you're coming with me no matter what," she said with confidence.

"FORGET THAT IM-" Cherry put a knife to my throat so fast I didn't even see her arm move. "You. Are. Going." She said with a serious tone.

"Y-You know what? I changed my mind. I'll go," I said in the best I didn't just pee my pants type voice.

"Great, the plan is set now. We will strike in four days. Prep yourselves. It's time to get a new base of operations... and a new bar." Cherry points to Steve's failure to make a mixed Vodka.

So, after another run-through of the plan and some terribly mixed drinks, we waited for the day of conquest; at least, that's what Cherry called it, even though it didn't really matter.

***

I was in my apartment, waiting for what was to come, and wondering what god I had been given a name for. I decided to look up more about Anubis. I found a Vokapideah about him: Anubis, the god of death, mummification, embalming, the afterlife, and the underworld.

I was mainly surprised he was a god, but it just helped me understand myself. I was still intrigued by his story. He went by different names, and he had many other shrines and stuff like that, but I had to stop because it seemed the walls were not soundproof, and let's just say my neighbors were making too much noise with their music.

After two days of rest, we were all called in unexpectedly to the shack, and I freaked out because I had never known I had a phone installed in my house until now. Wait, how do I know that? But Cherry distracted me from my thoughts.

"So why did you call us in Cherry, and how did you know my home number?" I said with curiosity.

"I called you all here because," she paused, "I was bored."

We all looked at her as if she were the most hated person in the world. "Why the hell would you do that?!" Lust yelled, "I was watching the Queen of Lust's livestream!" Lust said with anger.

"I was sleeping," Deviant said with annoyance.

"Yeah, and I was learning how to bake a cake!" Steve cried out in sadness.

"Wait, Steve, were you in the middle of making the cake?" I asked.

"Yeah, why?"

"No reason," I said nervously. Knowing what would happen when he got home. I think everyone knew what was going to happen.

Cherry sighed, "Anyway, another reason why I called you all here was to talk to you about this guy's training." pointing at me.

"Why me? I already know how to use my weapons." I said with confusion in my voice.

"Well, you may have efficiency with your weapons, but you don't know your *Special Skills*." She said it with the feeling of knowing the info, but I was still curious.

"So, what are these special skills?" I asked Cherry.

"Well, I'll show you," she said with enthusiasm.

"As you can see, I can change my voice; that's my power, but it does come with a side effect. I lose my voice for 2 minutes for every 1 minute I use my power."

I was surprised by the usage of her skills and the fact that they even exist. "Does everyone in this world have a skill?"She shook her head yes, implying that she couldn't use her voice.

Deviant and the rest told me about their powers and side effects. Deviant had a ghost-like power; he could be transparent and walk through walls, but the only problem was that his weakness made his thoughts audible to everyone within two yards when he stopped using it.

Lust can bring out anyone's deepest desires. But the stronger they resist, the greater the consequences. After usage, he is unable to feel emotion for 24 hours or 5 days. I know it doesn't sound like a weakness, but he says he goes out to a lot of social events.

Lastly, Steve can summon lightning with a voltage amount that can kill people. It can go on for as long as possible. The downside is that his weakness is more of a requirement, and he must be badly wounded or near death to activate it. However, the upside is the lighting heals him, but he still has lingering pain.

"So, what's my Power?" Everyone looked at me with curiosity.

"You don't know your own Power...?" Deviant asked with an annoyed face.

"Am I supposed to?" I said, confused.

Deviant slapped his face and said, "Everyone's powers activate after usually 2-3 days when they arrive in The Void, so just try to figure it out.

"Or~ we try to activate it forcefully," Cherry said in a cheerful tone, holding up a bat that was leaning against the desk. "I mean, it worked with Steve," Cherry said, pointing the bat at him. Steve recoiled and looked scared, then stood in front of me.

"Yes, it did, but in the process, I NEARLY FUCKING DIED." Cherry looked confused, as if this was a normal occurrence.

"Yeah, so what? At least you weren't killed, even though you can just reform," she said nonchalantly.

"Well, Lust and I are going to help him figure out his power," Steve said, sounding worried for me.

"K, see you guys in 2 days," Cherry said boringly.

I waved bye as we left the shack, and I immediately headed home. I knew I had training tomorrow and was somewhat excited about it. I still wondered; everyone's powers correlate with their names, so would mine be the definition of death?

But then I remembered Steve's name doesn't have any correlation to his power and went straight to sleep after quietly laughing my ass off about it for nearly an hour.

Chapter 3

The Power

I got up and went to Lust's place to train, and let's just say it was... interesting. If the Seven Deadly Sins and MAINLY The Queen of Lust had a fan, he would, no, not would; he IS the #1 Fan.

There were pictures of her everywhere, and he also had figurines of her as well. He had a body pillow of her, and that's not even the weird part. He had pictures of her in the bathroom, he, for some reason, has five different fragrances of her bath water (yes, they sell that shit here), and he had a whip she had used on sinners IN THE 90s on a frame- A FRAME!

The Den, his room, the bathroom, and other parts of the house I only caught glimpses of looked normal, but still, they had something relating to her, and I think I saw a Storage room! I didn't even ask-Steve changed the subject immediately.

"So, what would be one way for us to figure out Anubis's power?" Steve said, sounding curious and a little nervous.

"Well, we should first figure out if his power is a requirement type or side effect type.

I wondered what Lust meant when he said *requirement type*.

"What's a requirement type?" I asked.

"Well, it's like Steve's power; he needs to be Gravely wounded in order to use his power, and a common way to tell if it is a requirement is if it didn't activate after the first day in the void. But it doesn't mean you could be one."

"So pretty much, I was a requirement from the get-go. So, we need to determine what the requirement is."

I started to remember what I heard happened to Steve, and I got scared. I already died once, so why would anyone willingly experience it again. I began to fear what it would feel like.

"Well, sometimes people have certain things correlating to their powers, and since your name is related to the Egyptian god of death, let's go to the closest cemetery."

Now, I was surprised and said, "They have Cemeteries here?" Yes, but mainly, they are not made to bury dead bodies; instead, it's for those who cashed out, and no one wants to help pay for them to reform. It's sad but true; just because you can't die here doesn't mean you can die without a care in the world. It's still going to be like whatever life you lived on Earth, just without permanent death and more violence and capitalism.

So, we went to the closest cemetery, but here's the thing, Steve told me before we left that in The Void, you don't feel tired (stamina-wise), but you can still get fatigued. Of course, we still have cars, but it's useless since you could walk or run the number of miles it takes to get to the coffee shop down the road. Unfortunately, after 5 hours, we make it to the cemetery, and my body feels like it wants to die. "Why does my body hurt when I'm not even tired," I say on the ground, curled up in a ball.

"Well, it seems your little body is not used to the fatigue yet," Steve said, teasing me. "Well, my mind is used to your bullshit," I said, annoyed.

"Enough ladies, you're both beautiful right now; what we need to do is strategize," Lust said.

"Why strategize when all we need to do is to be in the environment," Steve said, pointing at me while looking out into the cemetery.

"I always wondered what powers are like in this world; I wonder what mine will be like," I said with curiosity, but I started to question myself: When did I start wondering why I say these things when I can't even remember my past life? I put it in the back of my mind to worry about later, along with other questions about this world. "So, what's the first thing on our list?" I asked with curiosity.

"Well, we planned three things to activate your powers, Lust stated.

1. Show you a dead body
2. Show you Blood
3. Kill someone or you.

The third one is a last resort," Lust said with a smile on his face.

I was so mortified my jaw was open as wide as it could be, and all I could say was, "HOW DID YOU SAY THAT SO CALMLY AND WITH A SMILE!?" I said with pure shock in my voice.

"Well, after being in The Void for over 100 years, you really get used to the stuff that happens here, including death," he said confidently.

"Bro, the only person here who has actually been here that long is Cherry," Steve said, calling Lust out for his lies. Lust stood there like a statue, slowly turning his head around. "It seems Number 1 will be done first," Lust says, trying to mask his anger, bloodlust, and a tiny bit of embarrassment.

Steve readied himself in a fighting stance, but Lust turned his head around, grabbed a shovel, went to a random grave, and started digging aggressively.

After 30 minutes of digging, he got the body out, and I felt nothing upon seeing it, so we went on to do number 2. I felt something churn in my stomach when I saw the blood, but I just assumed I was uneasy seeing blood. It felt like I was going to lose consciousness. So we decided we needed to prepare for Number 3. So, we took a break and agreed to meet up the next day.

We met up again, but this time at Steve's house. Now, I was expecting something bland, like his name, or something *crazy*, but instead, it looked like a regular place, like if you went into a house somewhere in the suburbs (other than the exploded oven in the kitchen with a perfect razzberry cake on the kitchen counter).

We sat down in his living room with Lust dressed to the 9s in his Crimson rose-colored suit (which was a part of the Queen of Lust's designer brands) and dark red dress shoes.

Steven came in with his usual blue shirt, blue jeans, and tennis shoes. *(why I'm saying their clothes, it will be important later)*

So, I told them about the feeling I had when I saw the blood.

"Well, when there's a requirement, you should usually feel something, so don't worry about it. Lust said.

Steve interjected, "It's like puberty but with powers. I feel it every time I die." He laughs while saying that, and I feel a little more relieved that there's someone who is somewhat similar to me, but I still feel our powers are different from one another —very different.

We went outside behind the apartment complex to test my power and see what it was. Lust and Steve stood behind a home-made defensive barrier 20ft away from me, made from wood and stone with some weird translucent black liquid on it.

Lust yelled, "YOU READY, ANUBIS?" I cried, "YEP, START THE TE-" before I could finish the sentence, a loud boom erupted. I blacked out and awoke to being restrained by both Lust and Steve, along with my body feeling strained.

"W-What's going on?!" I ask in a panic. Lust realizes it's me and lets go of my arms; seeing this, Steve freaks out and runs into a wall, knocking himself out.

I ask what happened, and Lust says that after they shot me, my body turned Pitch Black and with sharp thorns that appeared out of most of my body. I destroyed their barrier and nearly killed them, and that was all in within 30 minutes...

"30 MINUTES, I BLACKED OUT AND NEARLY KILLED YOU TWO IN 30 MINUTES?!"

I was freaking out, and Lust looked at me seriously and told me one more thing about what I looked like and told me not to use my power unless it was a last resort. "Your eyes looked so calm and cold."Lust said with fear in his voice, "It was as if you didn't care whether we were your friends, family, or enemy; you only saw us as an obstacle to your goal, whatever that was."

Those words shook me to my core.

Chapter 4

The Battle

The day finally came, and we all gathered around the table. Lust looked like he was auditioning for a military drag race (in all honesty, he still looks scary).

Steve was wearing an all-black suit, and he looked as though he hadn't slept a wink. When I came in, he jumped slightly but calmed down, saying, "Oh, thank god it's just you." It was just quiet enough so only lust and I could hear it.

Deviant had an all-black suit like Steve's, but from what I saw, he had one of those latex onesies at the top that people in spy shows would wear. Then there was Cherry, and I must say she looked really good in a Kevlar vest; she even had military clothes underneath it, complete with a helmet.

"So, did you figure out your power yet, Little J" Now, before I answered, I saw Lust staring at me, shaking his head no, so I changed the subject by asking about the nickname "Little J?" I said with confusion "Yea Anubis is an African Jackal so I thought Little J would fit you nice since your new here and all," she said with confidence. I didn't know that, but it still didn't make me like the nickname, nor was I against her using it because I thought it was clever.

Lust asked her if she could explain the plan again, and Cherry's eyes lit up as if she had been waiting for this moment. Even though we've only been gone for 4 days, which is close to a week, but still.

"So, the guard shift changes around 2:50. Lust needs to knock out the incoming guards, and with that, Steve and Deviant will post up, and while that's happening, me and Anubis will walk through the front gate with ease." Steve interrupts her, "If that's the case, what about the two other guards?" Cherry looked confused, then realized the issue and decided to change the plan slightly

"So after Steve and Deviant swap with the Two guards, Deviant will come around and knock them out, then hide them in the bushes-" Then Lust interrupted, asking, "But how will we all get inside to let you two in."

Cherry had a smirk, then lifted a weird-looking crystal. "WITH THIS," she said with proud confidence. Everyone had shocked looks on their faces, except for me, who was confused about what that object was. "So, what's that thing?" Almost everyone looked at me in anger. Deviant looked like he already knew I was going to ask the question.

Then Cherry stated..."Well, I'll tell you since you're new," she said with annoyance.

"This is a Teleport crystal, and it teleports you to wherever you placed the other crystal. I put the other one in a back alleyway deep enough so that nobody would find it." Deviant nodded in agreement.

It's very expensive, but it's worth it," she whispered.

"Can you reform?!" I asked immediately, worried after hearing it was expensive.

"Yeah, of course, I can reform; I still have like 70 dollars left, meaning I can reform 70 times," she says, but her body language said otherwise. Her hands were shaking like an earthquake. Then Deviant asked, "How much do you really have Cherry?" She started sweating and looked down, "10 dollars," she said quietly

"What was that, Cherry?" Deviant a- "10 DOLLARS A'RIGHT," she said so loud she interrupted the narration...{ *what a prick.*}

Everyone had looks of shock on their faces, "WHY WOULD YOU BUY SOMETHING LIKE THAT?! YOU CAN ONLY REFORM 10 TIMES NOW," Lust said, slightly freaking out

"I know, but I thought I had saved up enough money to reform a good amount."

Now, I didn't understand why having 10 lives was such a bad thing, but then I realized this is The Void. I'm guessing many people could care less about life since you can re-form as long as you have money. I reckon some people just kill to kill, meaning... if you leave outside your apartment with 1 dollar to your name, you won't just be homeless; you could be dead. *I mean, dead, until someone decides to pay you back to life, and even then, you better hope they leave insurance (like $ 30 to $ 40 extra) to let you earn it back.*

So, after realizing the situation, I yelled." WHAT IN THE EVER-DYING FUCK IS WRONG WITH YOU CHERRY!" Which everyone agreed with, and I was slightly surprised that I had caught on so quickly. "I know people like to buy stuff like Bluuci and Gouis Guitton, BUT THAT WOULD JUST MAKE YOU GO BACKUP, NOT BANKRUPT AND HAVE A CHANCE TO DIE!"

Cherry looked a little guilty. "Let's just focus on the plan and ignore the fact I have $10 to my name, please," she said in an embarrassingly quiet voice.

"We will use this crystal to Teleport me and Little J into the place after everything is in order. Then we will all place our flag In one of the buildings I scouted." She said confidently, "Then we just have to keep it safe for 10 minutes to claim it."

I was kind of surprised about how easy it sounded. "Why do we need to do all of that if all we have to do is keep a Flag safe for 10 minutes?" I asked curiously.

Cherry, in a militant stance, stated, "Oh? Well, because-

1.It sends out a massive alarm around the area

2 It reveals all our locations within the building for 10 Seconds, but our teammates will be teleported to the building we are trying to capture and

3 Those who participate in the capture, their reform time is doubled, and they reform inside the building until capture is over."

She said all of this while smiling as Steve turned off the mysterious speaker that had been playing military music.

Everything in me was both scared and freaked out by how calm Cherry was, along with everyone else. Well, except for Steve, who looked more worried than scared, especially when turning off the music.

"So, now that everyone has the rundown of the plan, ARE WE ALL READY TO GET OUR NEW BASE!!" We all shook our heads in agreement, and I felt a little excited about the fact I was about to prove my worth to the team... and to get a new place than this rusty old shed.

A few Hours Later (you know the voice)

So, the first part of the plan was in action, but there was one problem.

"So how much longer before the switch," Steve said uncomfortably. He and Deviant were in the bushes a few meters away from the guards.

"Cherry said that they swap at 2:50, so it's expected if they are a little late."

"What time is it now?" Steve asked Deviant

"It's 2:49," and right as he said that, two guards arrived, and they switched.

Two minutes later, Steve asked again knowingly.

"What time is it?"

Deviant looked at his watch 2:52. "What the fuck!!" Deviant said in a loud whisper while pulling out his radio, "Lust, what are you doing right now? The guards you were supposed to knock out are still here." Deviant said in a confused panic.

"Sorry, sweetie, but I need to relax," said Lust in a slurred manner.

"Lust... are you fucking drunk?" Deviant asked Lust annoyingly.

"Yep, and I think you need to come ov-"

Deviant interrupts Lust, "If you don't get your sorry ass to our location right fucking now, I'm burning that limited edition Queen Of Lust Body pillow when it gets to your house."

Lust snaps out of his drunkenness instantly, and you can hear him on the radio

running out of the bar to their location immediately.

"Since Lust is being useless right now, I'll
use my power to knock out the guards and
put them in the bushes. Then you come over,
we open the gate, and then we pretend to
watch the gate till they place the flag down.
So, Steve, you stay here."

Deviant disappears from Steve's sight before he can even blink, and 30 seconds later,
Steve sees the two guards' radios float, then
drop to the ground, and their bodies float to
the bushes, all in the span of two minutes.
Deviant slowly reappeared, signaling Steve to
come over.

"How did you do that so quickly?" Steve
asked Deviant, and all Deviant said was "my
past life," which only intrigued Steve more.
However, he was interrupted by Cherry,
standing at the gate with Anubis right behind
her. They opened the gate so they could
come in as the Second stage of the plan came
to fruition.

Chapter 5

Capture the Flag

Cherry, Steve, Deviant, and I were standing at the gate, preparing for the next part of the plan. "So, how was your part of the plan?" Cherry asked with curiosity.

"Well, Lust went to a bar and decided to get drunk, which is why I had to use my ability and knock out the two guards," Deviant said with annoyance.

"Oh, so that's why Lust isn't here yet... where is he anyway," Cherry asked Deviant.

"I don't know; all I remember is hearing him run out of a bar on his radio after I told him to get his behind over here or I'd burn the body pillow he ordered," Deviant said, "and now we are just waiting for him to get here."

Cherry and I both looked slightly annoyed, but Cherry looked more mad than annoyed.

"Alright then, I guess we will go hide in those bushes till he gets here," and right as she finishes her sentence, he comes around the corner and goes all the way up the hill to join the group.

"Am I late?" said Lust, out of breath and sweating from head to toe, "Oh no, you're not late," said Cherry in a Cheerful tone "Oh, thank go-" "YOU ARE CLOSE TO LEAVING THE FREAKING TEAM" Lust was interrupted by a furious Cherry she looked like she was going to tear his head off, so much so that Steve and Deviant were ready to tackle her down till she calmed down.

"Look, as much as I want to release my anger on you, I'm going to let it slide, but just know if you mess up any other part of this plan, I will make you wish you were never sent here."

Cherry said that last part with such coldness that it felt like she was talking to all of us, not just Lust.

So, we all walked our way to the building. I didn't know why everyone didn't notice us or find us suspicious. "Hey, Deviant, why is nobody asking us questions or wondering why we're here?" I asked, and he looked at me with a minimal amount of excitement in his eyes.

"Well, when people enter another person's area, they are unable to be heard or seen unless- they attack someone that lives within the territory- or announce themselves to someone within the territory. But People can be able to see them if they are looking for someone outside the area, which will make it where they are visible to that person."

It confused me, but I got the gist of it and wanted to test it out. I tried to touch one of the guys in suits, but Deviant grabbed my wrist before I could even touch him and stared me down like a parent about to discipline their child.

"Did you not listen to what I just said? They will immediately attack us if you announce yourself like that," Deviant said in a semi-quiet voice. I tugged my hand several times to break free from his grip, which was very strong and required seven tugs to break. I then continued walking with the rest of the group to our destination, feeling a little annoyed about what he had done.

"Here we are, the building I've been scouting out for weeks now," Cherry said excitedly. We were all shocked and baffled at the House. Checking it out, it had a pool in the backyard, a minibar in the garage, and a weapon storage room in the attic, filled to the brim with guns.

"This place is nice, Cherry," Said Lust, surprised.

"Who owns it?" Steve asked Cherry.

"Oh, my Ex-Boyfriend," Cherry said sarcastically.

Now, I thought that stealing her ex-boyfriend's house was fine until I looked around and wondered why everyone was as stiff as a mannequin.

"Hey Cherry, why does everyone look like they saw Medusa?" I asked, not fully understanding the situation.

"Oh, they're just scared because he's an Angel," she said nicely.

I didn't think anything was wrong until I slowly realized something: this is the judgment ground of Heaven and Hell... WHAT WOULD HAPPEN IF YOU ANGERED AN ANGEL? Different thoughts went through my mind, like would I be sent to Hell if he found out I was a part of this? Is he able to just kill me outright and ignore the reform timer? How in the ever-dying Frick did Cherry date an Angel? As those thoughts entered my mind, I became just as still as everyone else and was terrified for my semi-alive life.

So, after we were all well-prepared for the Capture of Cherry's ex-boyfriend's house, we were all trying to ignore the fact that her Ex is an angel and that he wouldn't try to attack *us within ten minutes of his house being taken.*

"Ok, I'm about to place down the flag. Are you guys ready?"

We all nod in agreement, and just as the flag touches the ground, "Oh yeah, I forgot to tell y'all if it's an Angel or Demons building or area, then the time doubles from 10 minutes to 20, and everyone becomes our enemy good luck," Cherry said cheerfully.

"WHAT!?" We all shouted just before we saw the timer above the flag show twenty minutes instead of ten. We were all freaking out over the fact that she just tricked us into Capturing the house of an Angel. Still, Deviant ran immediately toward the window, "Guys, you should come look at this."

We all go to the window. At the same time, Cherry loads her guns, and we see at least 60 people outside, along with a timer that is counting down from 5 minutes.

We all went from freaking out to imme-diately preparing for battle. Running around like chickens with their heads cut off.

- Steve was grabbing and throwing knives.
- Deviant was checking the ammo for his sniper
- Lust was putting silencers on his Pistols.

All the while, I did nothing but polish my Scythe and Guns and count the ammo in the attic.

Out of everyone, me and Cherry were not frantic. We were as calm as can be.

I understood that Cherry expected this, but I was surprised by how calm I remained in the face of danger. For some reason, I wanted the time to end sooner, just so I wouldn't have to prepare for battle.

I wanted to fight, to ki- my thought inter-rupted.

"Hey, Anubis, the timer is almost up. Go to Steve," Deviant said as he moved to his perch.

It seems I had zoned out while polishing my scythe, and the timer went down by 4 minutes.

"I'm coming down now," I said while picking up my weapons. As I came down the ladder, I saw numerous defensive weapons, including turrets peeking through the windows, traps with spikes at the bottom, and even a place to snipe on the roof for Deviant to take people out from a distance.

"Hey Steve, won't they see the traps outside and mostly avoid them along with Deviant's sniper perch," I asked Steve, wondering if everything they did was for nothing.

"Well, actually, they can't see anything we do in here, so we can lay traps and such. "

I was surprised, but I also knew it would be a good idea to take advantage of that.

"Plus, Cherry will be in the attic with a minigun, just in case they get past us," Steve said with one-sided confidence- praying they would not get past us.

As I watched Steve silently pray, I offered him some advice...

"Yeah, all I'm going to say to you is don't let your guard down," I said to Steve while the timer counted down from 1 minute before the battle started.

I asked Steve as I stood in front of the door.

"Ok, so what's the plan?"

"Well, we're all just gonna use guns and try to stay away from dying so none of us lose our lives and reform, just so you know," Steve said. I felt like that would be boring, so I decided to go out there as soon as the force field dropped.

"Ten seconds left, get ready," Deviant said over the radio. As I readied my scythe for battle, everyone outside the force field appeared to be preparing their weapons and many other things, too. But for some reason, while everyone looked nervous, I felt that this was normal. The timer hit Zero, and the moment the force field went down, I ran straight outside and was immediately bombarded with bullets. But my body moved on its own as if it were instinct.

I threw my scythe while dodging the bullets, and it was thrown with such strength that it went through at least ten of them. I immediately switched to my Pistols and ran to get cover inside the house while providing cover for myself and taking out another three. I dived through the door and landed face-first on the floor; my scythe was right in front of me.

"Activate the TURRETS," I yelled at Lust as he was standing there, slack-jawed. "Y-yes, sir," Lust said as he pressed the buttons for the turrets to pop up from the ground and provide fire so we could strategize our next course of action.

"Ok, before y'all ask any questions about what happened out there, how is my scythe inside the house?" I asked because I was confused; I threw it toward the enemy. I had no way to collect it, so how is it inside the house?"

"Well, that's because if someone touches a weapon owned by someone else, it goes back to its owner unless the owner is uncon- scious or they give that person permission," Lust said, still shocked at the fact that I took out that many people.

"Now tell us how you did that when you never even fought before," Steve said with pure curiosity.

I was shocked myself; it felt like I wasn't in control of my body, or at least, it felt like in- stinct took over. "I don't know, but we should focus on the mission at hand. How much time did I buy us," I asked Deviant while I an- swered Steve's question.

"Well, with the 5 minutes that were taken off for preparing plus the fact you took out at least 22% of their group, plus Cherry's ex hasn't appeared yet, then we should have at least 10 minutes. That's also if two of the turrets don't get jammed," Deviant said through the radio, and pretty much it allowed us five minutes to rest."

Everyone started celebrating until Deviant heard it through the radio and told everyone to stop.

"Hey, Lust, I have something to tell you before the time is up," I said after I turned off my radio. "What's up, Little J, do you want a beer too?" Lust said, ignoring Deviants order to stop celebrating

"I'm gonna use my power if Cherry's Ex gets here or if there are more enemies than we can handle."

Lust's face changed from drunken happiness to a serious expression in an instant. "Are you sure you can control it?" Lust asked like a mom worrying for their child

"No, but If things go south, you know what to do: try to either restrain me or knock me out," I said with confidence that it would bring us to victory.

"Look, Anubis, I will tell you this much: if you go berserk, Steve and Cherry might try to restrain or knock you out, but Deviant will kill you on the spot, so I suggest you think about it," Lust said with bone-chilling seriousness and slight worry. He looked like he was gonna cry.

"2 minutes left before you have to go back out there, Anubis. Make sure to use the turrets as cover," Deviant said over the radio.

"Also, turn your radio back on, Anubis. I don't know why you turned it off, but we need to be informed about everything both inside and outside the house, and we still don't know how long it takes for your reform." I grabbed my weapons, reloaded my guns, prepared extra ammunition, and readied myself for the next fight.

"1 minute!" Deviant said over the radio, "Hey, Lust, just know it's only a last resort. I'm not gonna use it immediately, and I'm not gonna die easily," I yelled to Lust from across the house, assuring him I wouldn't try to use my power unless something interrupts our main plans. "Alright, good luck then, and make sure to take all of them out," Lust yelled back, smiling. "No promises." "5 seconds!" Deviant said over the radio, "4, 3, 2, 1, Now!"

I ran out the door toward a turret that was still firing while the rest were cooling off, and right as I got to it, the turret stopped firing. Two soldiers tried to advance on me, but they fell into two of the pitfalls, and five more fell into them, except for one. My instincts took over and shot him when he came around the corner before he could react.

This was the first time I actually saw what happens when someone dies. His body turned to dust, and I just kept shooting and reloading for at least another 5 minutes, keeping my desire to fight repressed so I didn't go overboard and start using my scythe.

"The Turrets are done cooling. Anubis, get back inside as soon as you can," Deviant said.

"Ok, well, can you deal with the HEAVY FIRE ON MY AZZ" I shouted into my radio. I could hear Cherry's laugh from the house after shouting that, but I didn't care; I was too angry and blood-lusty to care.

"Try to get out like you did last time. I can't snipe as fast as they shoot." I was annoyed, but I just ran for the door. It seemed my body was tired, and I couldn't run as fast, so I got shot in both my legs. I fell to the ground, and I saw a guy aiming his gun at my head, and I died.

I immediately woke up. Steve seemed to have turned around to look at me; his face was in utter shock. "I guess I died; how long was I out," I asked Steve, who was still too stunned to talk to me.

"I'll... answer for him," Lust said. "You were dead for 2 seconds."

Now I was laughing. I thought they were joking with me; the shortest recorded time was 10 minutes.

"Ok, ok, funny joke, but how long was I really dead," I asked seriously.

Their facial expressions didn't change, which meant I had the fastest recorded reform time within the history of The Void.

Chapter 6

The Guardian Angel

We go to the window to see a man with two beautiful, blinding white wings floating down to the ground. "Who is that?" I asked Deviant through my radio, "That's Cherry's Ex." Deviant said right behind me.

I didn't even notice him or hear any Noise. "Luckily, we only have 4 minutes left, so we might not have to fight him." I was so focused on Cherry's ex that I forgot we were trying to capture his house. "Ok... we're dead, right," I said with a blank expression, as everyone else faces looked like they agreed.

"Nope, Because I have a plan," Cherry said, coming down the stairs. "Ok, it's not throwing me off the roof. Near-death right," Steve said, annoyed at the thought of it.

Cherry looked like she was caught Red-Handed. "W-H WHAT NO~" Cherry said loudly.

"I had something entirely different than that." She took a moment to think and then pointed at me. "Little J will fight him," She said confidently. Then Lust exclaimed, "NO! I was fine with everything else, Cherry, but I'm not letting him die again, even if he can reform in 2 seconds," he said with a lot of emotion.

I stood there listening, unsure why he was acting this way, but I let them fight it out while I planned how I would fight the angel if it came down to it.

"Wait, Anubis can reform in 2 seconds?" Deviant said in disbelief

"Oh, I forgot to tell you, Steve interrupted us before we could. Yep, Little J, here is now the fastest person to reform in The Void,"

Cherry said. "Plus, I'm thinking we just keep sending him out there as bait to keep him preoccupied. You know how much he loves to play around with us," Cherry said cheerfully. "If playing around with us means tearing us limb from limb, then sure, go ahead and send someone," Lust said sarcastically.

I could feel the motherly protection emanating from Lust, and all I could think of was finding the weak points on the angel... *WHY WAS LUST MOTHERLY screamed in my head? Other than that, my thoughts were analyzing the angel. For the entire time since the angel landed, he was planted in the same spot. I think two minutes have passed. I don't know why he's standing there. Maybe he's waiting for us to come out of the house, or perhaps he just likes looking like a mannequin for fun.*

"Sooo, have you guys decided whether or not I'm going to be cannon fodder to this guy or what? Because I don't think he will let us get out of here alive," I said, looking for an escape route.

As we looked outside, we noticed that none of the enemies were shooting, nor were they doing anything at all. They aren't even trying to advance when they know they have the advantage.

"I want to test something," Deviant said while opening the door. He threw one of his magazines for his sniper into the open, and within the blink of an eye, the angel pulled out his gun and shot it. When we got a good look at it, the bullet had gone straight through it.

"Ok, so Anubis has to fight someone whose guns can literally put holes into his body."

"NOPE, HES NOT GOING OUT THERE!" Lust said, more determined than he ever was to keep me from dying again in front of his eyes.

I understood why he didn't want me out there, but I also wanted to fight the angel. Every-thing within my body screamed to fight him. Still, I already know that if I do, there's a big risk I'll die unless....

"Lust, If I use my power, do you think I could stand a chance against him," I asked, hoping that might give him some relief.

"Yes, you could, but I still will not allow you to go out there and die again." Lust looked like a mom who was trying to keep their child from danger, but they kept going towards it. "Please, Anubis, don't go out there. We can find another way."

Deviant interrupted and said, "There is no other way; the only two plans we have are going out there and dying to him or two-..."

Deviant was interrupted by a loud beeping noise in the attic. So we went to check. At the same time, Steve stayed downstairs to watch the angel. When we reached the attic, the timer had reached zero. Our base was officially now the house.

"So I guess we live here now," I said in an unbelieved tone.

"Nope, it just copied the place," said Cherry. "Now, when we go back home, we won't see the shed. We will see this place," Cherry said gleefully; I was confused, but before I could ask any questions, Cherry started pushing me toward exiting the attic.

"Now, onto sending you out there," Chery stated, but Lust stood in my way

"I've already told you I'm not letting him go out there."

I grew tired of Lust keeping me from fighting or, at the very least, getting everyone to safety.

"Lust, I will go out there, and I'll use my power. Everyone else try to sneak out the back- while I try to fight him."

"Can you guys also take my scythe so I don't lose it? I'll use one of my pistols so I can activate the power. I suggest you move as far away from me as possible. I'm not sure if my plan will work or if I can control it."

Steve and Lust understood what I meant; Deviant was curious, and Cherry didn't know why.

When I got downstairs. I stood in front of the door and prepared myself to dodge the bullets.

"Are you sure about this, Anubis?" Deviant said on the radio

"Nope, but at least if I die, I'll Reform," I said with confidence. "

"Good luck, Anubis, and don't die, alright?" Lust said on the radio.

"I'll do my best."

I ran out the door and went for cover. I heard the bullets but didn't see the angel pull out his gun. Luckily, I found cover behind one of the turrets before he could actually hit me, but I was grazed on my left leg. Seeing the blood slightly triggered my power, but I needed it to be stronger. So I peeked around the corner and started provoking the guy by shooting him.

But he grabbed all of my bullets like he was in the matrix.

So instead, I ran at him and got shot in the same leg, and this time, seeing the blood spew out allowed me to activate my power, Although only some of it. It felt like my Instincts but more wild and free. The good news is that my wounded leg regenerated.

However, the angel tried to shoot me again. His movements felt more on par with mine, so I dodged it.

My instincts took over for a second, and I attacked him with a punch that knocked him back at least three houses away. I was shocked, the good kind of shock that makes you think, 'That was awesome.'

I saw him fly towards me; I ducked. He pulled out his gun again and took two shots, both hitting my trapezoids.

I expected to have two holes in my body, but instead, a black slime-like entity appeared and protected me from the shots. So I taunted him, "HA! Not so brave without your bullets now-"

But before I could finish the sentence, I turned to see an army of guns floating around the angel in midair. I immediately ran towards the house and made it just as the heavy fire from the guns rained down upon me.

As I was catching my breath, I heard him saying something in German. I couldn't understand him, but I understood two words, "or" and "nice." So I'm guessing he's trying to negotiate or asking me to surrender, so I responded with, "I don't speak Gibberish, so can you please speak a more common language?" The firing slowed down, and the angel said, "Please surrender, or I will not be so merciful."

As I was about to look around the corner to respond with some form of eye contact, my instincts pulled me back just in time. The angel stopped only to speak, then continued the onslaught. As the heavy fire continued. So I, Anubis, yelled out (I just wanted to say that now, back to the story).

"Sorry, but I can't really do that. You see, My instincts have been looking to fight someone strong, and for some reason, you're it." I said confidently

"So I'm gonna fight you and most likely die trying, but I also can't die because I made a promise, so I'm gonna have to decline your surrender." He seemed to start laughing

"Damn, you are one stubborn human, I will face you one on one then," he said with a smile on his face as he stopped the gunfire.

I came from around the side of the house, only to see all the guns fall to the ground.

"Are you still confident you can fight me and live human?" he asked curiously.

"Of course I am, but winning will be determined through our battle," I said with confidence. We both waited for someone to make the first move; it seemed we had the same thought in mind - *the person who makes the first move will decide the fate of the battle.*

I ran at him and threw a punch, but he dodged it. I ducked instantly as he punched me and grabbed me by the shoulders; his knee met my stomach. "Augh," and I was knocked back a few feet.

My instincts kicked in, and I started dodging most of his attacks, not all of them, but most. I tried to make as much distance as possible, but it was no use. Every time I tried to step back, he came at me as fast as he could and punched me. I tried to dodge most of them successfully, but some punches still grazed or hit me. I became a punching bag with powers, trying to find the angel's weakness, any weakness to throw him off guard, giving me an advantage. He was attacking me so frequently that I couldn't find a moment to breathe.

"WHAT'S WRONG, HUMAN? I THOUGHT YOU WERE CONFIDENT IN DEFEATING ME!" He said joyfully as I was dodging his attacks.

I decided to test the range of my powers. I lifted my hand and said, "TAKE THIS, YOU LOUSY ANGEL." Suddenly, a man appeared from the ground. He looked like he was from America, with a USA Cap on, bandages all over his body, and a Kevlar vest. He was holding a rifle, although I didn't know what kind.

"OH, MY FATHER, DID YOU REALLY SUMMON A HUMAN TO FIGHT FOR YOU?" He was laughing so hard that I thought he was going to die. Of course, I tried to punch him while his guard was down, but he just grabbed my fist and punched me in the gut.

I flew towards the guy I summoned, but I landed on the ground instead of the guy. I looked around, and the next thing I know, the guy I had summoned was right behind the angel.

The angel immediately pulled out his gun. Without looking behind him, he shot the guy in the head. "Did he really think that could defeat me? What a waste," the angel gloated, but suddenly the guy, *I'm naming him Dave from now on...* picked up his gun, and shot the angel in the back. Dave continued to shoot at him, but the angel used his wings to protect himself. I decided to try to summon more, but only three more came out of the ground.

However, it seemed to be more than enough. As the angel was being pummeled with bullets, I noticed he mainly used his wings for protection. This gave me an idea; I ran towards the guys who were just watching from the sidelines, grabbed one of their grenades, and threw it at him. he blew the four guys I summoned away, each one turning to dust in midair. The grenade landed right underneath his feet. "YOU SHOULD LOOK DOWN, DUMMY."

He looked to see the grenade just as it exploded. It seemed he had used his wings to shield himself from the explosion, but they were partly burned and damaged in the process. I ran at him and threw a haymaker at his face. I was finally landing some hits. I kicked as high as I could in the air and immediately flew after him to kick him to the ground. He tried to use his broken wings to dodge, but it just spun him around in the air. I used that moment to grab one of his wings and kick him back to the ground.

"It seems I've found your weakness. Your wings are the only line of defense to protect yourself," I said mockingly as I floated back down. The angel made a weird movement with his hands, then he ran up and tried to punch me. I knocked him to the ground, he said something under his breath, everything went black.

"It seems I've found your weakness. Your wings are the only line of defense to protect yourself, I said mockingly. The angel made a weird movement with his hands, then he ran up and tried to punch me. *Hang on, why does this feel familiar? I thought,* along with the protagonist.

So, I decided not to knock the angel to the ground. I took two steps back, and he kept trying to hit me, but I just kept dodging because I felt like something was off about this fight. I decided to test it by punching him, then everything went black. I was back to the moment I took my first two steps. I realized the angel was sending me back a few seconds in time to give himself the upper hand, but I didn't know what was triggering the time reversal.

Suddenly, I hear a voice...."What's wrong? Starting to feel weak?" I looked around but didn't see anyone. "Who's there? If you're an ally help me; if not, back the F' off," I said while trying to figure out the voice's location and intentions. *Wouldn't you know it? I was hearing voices in my head because the angel was still attacking me.*

Then I heard the voice again... "Well, the angel seems to be a distraction let me help out with that." A black goo emerged from my body and immobilized him. "This won't hold for long, but I will tell you this before I go just to see if you accept my deal. I'll give you my power to defeat this angel," the voice said happily.

I was confused, and it felt very sketchy. I asked, "What's in it for you," I asked to hear its reaction. "You are a smart human, but I will not do you any harm. All I want is a new place to call home, which would be your body," the female voice said. I was considering whether to accept, but as I thought about it, the angel got up and impaled me through the chest.

So, as I was hovering with the angel's hands through my chest around my heart, I yelled. "I'LL ACCEPT YOUR DAMN DEAL!" A black substance starts to surround me like a cocoon, and in the last moments, I hear her voice before I am fully submerged, "Welcome again to the world of death itself, your grace."

TO BE CONTINUED

Words from the Author

Let's keep this simple—because I'd rather be asleep right now. I started writing this novelette when I was 12, mostly because my brain decided it had something to say (for once). I'm a fan of manhwa, gaming, and weird facts that make people pause mid-conversation. Life is strange, and I like to study the parts most people skip over. I'm not trying to be deep, but the world is huge, and we're just poking at it with a stick. I write stories because sometimes that stick hits something interesting.